MUT

BRENDAN McNAMEE

Published by Blunt Films Ltd 2014 ©
First available September 2014

www.bluntfilms.co.uk
twitter.com/brendanmcnamee

Design by www.greg-stevenson.co.uk

ISBN 978-0-9930225-0-0

For my mother who fosters a love of dogs and books.

U.

The city hunched around the beach like a protective
father. Cracks in the *pavé* tracing stories.
A crackle-lure heart that beat irregularly with old age.
A most beautiful hell. A sinful stack of angels.

Garbage rotting on the street corners. The
sickness and waste concentrated in piles. Still, I am
unable to quell the incessant tick of the metronome in
my eyes, my heart, my balls. It was the women. The fifth
and most important element. As the patriarch watches
over them, even those who come to trade the bags of
garbage on the beach float from receptacle to receptacle.
Lithe, brown arms lost in their oversized high visibility

tabards. Coconuts dropped by a lazy Aphrodite. The shape of every creature padding the boardwalk and laying prone to soak up the good Mediterranean sun. Perfect, fashioned by the largest of left-sided brains. This is where I would never, never, always forget her.

All downhill to the beach. A Brazilian strip heaves with near naked-husky maids. The shepherd, a proud septuagenarian on the cusp of the 'clothing optional' section. This sentry, bald and naked, proud and statuesque, gay or straight, he is the zest amongst the sweets. The tourist who did not double take him could be forgiven for mistaking him for art. A masterpiece hewn from bronze and placed with his back to the sea. His pizzle shrivelled and unused, the last thing you notice as if to spring the sale on you with a surprise. A second-hand car yard with one left on the lot. He keeps his eyes fixed on the trickle of tourists for the right sap to buy his junk, so he can pack it in and head for the hills.

The rats, hunting for carrion amongst the wrappers and the rocks, never getting caught by the waves. Locals flip beer caps at them, mocking with false sustenance. Jay birds circle relentlessly to break up the constant blue above. Tiny flocks of clouds. Their only objective to provide fleeting moments of shade that you could chase if you had the legs. A city de-sensitised to nudity as if long ago their gardens had been filled with rosy apples unbitten, serpents bored by the inaction. This constant stream of skin never ceases to delight. Like the glimmer of wonder on Charlie Bucket's face when he realises the river he glides along is made from chocolate. In a constant state of awe waiting for when the atoms will slow. Whether the sun, the water and the women will stop fizzing inside, so shook up like soda that I can come to rest in a warm, flat state.

Flat pop.

Settle the stomach.

Ease the nerves.

Attract the wasps.

I have one role. I wait... wait for the role in this world to be finished before I can contemplate moving onto the next.

Feeling like an old lady who constantly hears mysterious intruders.

Viewing the world through a crack in the curtain.

Projecting my life through those that I witness.

Judging them behind ten euro shades.

Never doing the same thing twice.

Slightly altering the routine, in case I'm being watched.
Up there, if you would like to direct your attention and
follow my pointed index finger skyward. There are
those in the board room at the top of the world. A coffee
with three sugars on day one, without any sugar on day
two. Waiting at the stripes with the tourists or crossing
a block up earlier than one needs. Waiting five minutes
extra before leaving the large, lonely life raft of a bed.

Sometimes I smoke a cigarette at noon on the
corner opposite the terrace, sometimes near the stair in
the shade. Chewing rather than sucking on a cheap blue
lollipop, a red one, a green one. Additives no fruit, no
minerals, just hue and saturation. Each day I must send
out a different volume of dots and dashes. I must confuse
the patterns, mix in the messages with the white noise.
Save my soul. Rescue my mind. Straddle the cusp. No
rhythm to the usual rhyme, no reason to the song. A
heartbeat mistimed and without the excuse of jazz. At
once out of breath and at rest. Coiled like a spring and
stretched taut and thin. Strong as steel, the breaking
tension of twine, I will not make *it* easy for them. They
fucked me once. Whoever they are. The collective, there

4

can surely be no one God to blame. Whatever *it* might turn out to be, I'll be the sort of man to take *it* on the chin.

I'll pull out the sleeve. Come read my open book written in lemon juice, like the old spies used to. It's all here to see, if you know how. I've been here a while, it could be longer, damn I could have been here even less. Poble-sec, the old part of town, the foot of the mountain. The cemeteries and the forest slope gently away above the tight streets and tapas bars. An authentic and narrow slice of Catalonia, the 'dry town'. Here they know me as well as any man can.

"*Mut*"

I hear them mumble to each other. "El Mut" 'The mute.'
I never speak to them. It suits my mood. It suits what's left inside. I don't want to hear that voice again... sure I'm not able to. I used to pretend, used to be polite. Make smiles with my eyes and hands. Apologise for my lack of skills. Now I am *mudo,* I'm *mut*. I have become one of them. Distinguishable from the *guiri* who walk their

quiet streets orientating maps like steering wheels. There is affection in their voices when they call out to me. I'm not deaf. Understanding the local dialect passes enough that the nods and smiles are genuine. Sunglasses afford a view on the world unaffected by judgement. Like a dog who watches the neighbour's cat through a well shaded ear from under the coolness of the porch. Both the cat and the dog know that no one is asleep, but they play along, adapt their roles and call time out for siesta.

When did it first happen? When did I first trade my voice for the keen hearing of the hound? Hard to pinpoint... sometime after she left and a little bit before I arrived. The two are connected, like putting gas into the tank helps you go, go, go. I understand the connection, but don't ask me to explain the workings of the internal combustion engine. Let's just say there is a trade-off, put in the gas, move it along, out comes the smoke.

Dos.

Sometime after she left me, she took that part
of me that she had made her own.
A space as big as a concert hall and yet
somehow she could palm with ease. Sometime
around then my voice went with her. As if
she had wrapped it in a handkerchief with
my heart and tied it to a stick. The dirt road
stretched to the horizon in front of her. She
had so much potential I didn't begrudge her
that voice. I wouldn't have begrudged her
anything she wanted. But as she left and my
heart became smaller, became nothing much
more than the speck she was on the plain.
I began to hear them. Mutts, pups, hounds,
canines, dogs, pooches. I became one of the

pack, as if I had always been part of their
litter. Did you ever smile at a baby and ignore
its mother? Did you ever have that connection
with just you two? It's real. That little child
stares deep into you, it sees you as darkness or
light and reacts accordingly.

For me, an animal lover, it's the same with dogs.
They know it, they notice me coming, watching like
builders hearing the click of a grand pair of heels down
the street. Dogs ain't much for whistling, but they sure
do undress you in their own way.

A dog is a dog is a dog. You can't teach an old
dog new tricks. It's raining cats and dogs. Dog eat dog.
This is what they say, if you ask a dog they say different.
They couldn't be more honest with you. A somewhat
princely life, never to be king. Sniffing an ass to find
where a fellow has been... whether they are formidable,
trustworthy, below or above you in society. Is this not a
more wholesome compromise than asking, "What school
did you attend? What do you do for a living? Is this your
wife?" If people are so inclined to know such things,
then why not smell my ass to find out. A fair trade. Being
a dog is so perfect, so simple. Licking one's own testi,

burying your nose in the crotch of a stranger, getting a kick in the ribs from one's own master. Pleasure and pain, a fair trade. If you are going to get a kicking from your master, better to know his face, better to bite the hand that feeds you than rail desperately at an omnipotent being hidden in the rays of the sun, behind clouds, deities or spires.

Each week, scattered amongst the nymphs I would count four specific women. I don't want you thinking I am 'that sort of boy.' The thing is… there is nothing as beautiful as a woman, nothing that you can eat that smells good enough to make you forget a woman and nothing that *feels* will make your life better than the fusion of your epidermis to their own. There were repeats, patterns. One I would cradle by the clock if I had the time. Two that I might chide for losing their looks. Muttering that the gift they were blessed with had been partied away. Drunk into oblivion, unwashed, unloved by themselves. Such a shame. I could paint them with my eyes shut, could see the beauty they had left without a custodian and subsequently lost. Every month without trying, I would find one like my mother. Still it would turn my feelings like a pancake in the air.

Something in her manner, her kindness that made me
see the woman I loved more than any other. There was
a duty, a repetition in seeing her. This stranger was my
Sunday roast. I wanted to gift her something, some love?
Crossing the street in front of the old woman so a car had
to slow and made her life a tiny bit easier. A Hail Mary
in her name, for although I am not religious there is no
doubt that each of these surrogates is. Reaching a box of
crackers for her on the top shelf. Cost me nothing but the
time I have in excess. Paying her back in instalments for
all the years of love and pocket money.

    I crave the man I once was, might have been
once more. A long ago dead twin that never made it out
of the womb and forever followed on my shoulder. Long
before I barked, before I was lost and shuffled through
the sun light. Long before the meaning of patience came
upon me in a gentle epiphany and the ways to maim
and kill a man in forty seven distinct fashions revolved
through the mind like a salad spinner. This man that I
once was, all mouth, no trousers, with the propensity for
violence which sits at the bottom of the pool of every
fellow. The seed of it just beneath the topsoil of the
psyche. A man throwing litter, speaking roughly to his

mutt, letting the door slam in the face of a lady. Those who would never say thank you those who'd never give space, push, expect to take and turn their blinkers on. Bankers who grabbed and grabbed. Politicians and Police. Child molesters and Property Magnates. All of them push the mercury in my blood to boiling. Always it was they who deserved a violent death, an unlucky death, Darwin's magic in a black cloak. I could never ignore them and just let go. They had to get to me. I had to slap the car, cheek the pig, throw the egg, give the finger. But never did I curl my fist so it was one cold bludgeon and use it spring like, to pulp a man. Once upon a time there were limits.

All that – so long ago. Back then, friends and lovers were as inseparable as two sides of a coin, even more so in a note, all folded, touching each other inside and out. A mess of limbs curled and sprayed, trusted, connected… gone now. All dead to me. Not their fault, kick that complaint up to the boardroom.

As a basket of wormholes can be no time at all and all the time in the world. There was once a moment I was nothing but potential in an empty hat. There was that second before I met her, not so dissimilar to the point

that chromosomes feted the sex of me. I could have been
anything. The possibility of an island nation soaked
in oil and without a king. The pass not yet dynamited
by a grinning engineer. The heart that beat inside my
chest was more innocent than a girl guide in bobby
socks hawking fresh cookies. I'd have stared down the
watchful gaze of a traffic cop with an ounce of California
cheese in my pack, sat in any seat of the airplane with a
giant fuck you to fate.
All this in the days before I met her.

Met Ana.

Sweet and brighter than sugar glass. That moment before
I saw her, I was king of the castle, ruled the world.
The second after, I knew I was nothing. Here was true
royalty. I was but a serf, a knave, a jack of fools. As
if from nowhere the fluids had been cleared from my
airways, my ass smacked and my nose pointed at her.
Now you're born.

The moment our eyes met, my first moment
of existence. She pinched me hard with that first smile
and when I awoke I knew I would forever rub the spot.

A common name, yet I had never seen it float in the air quite so. Spelt with one N in the mind but with two on her passport. She could have been called 'it' or 'a' and the vision that shaped the cursive would have looked so different from any other. 'Anna' she had spoken up. 'Ana' had rested next to the ferociously pumping engine. It was smaller, more befitting of her... an elf a nymph, a mouse, a bird. Turn her upside down, fold her in half, she'd be just as small. She was as unique as each breath drawn. If she smiled in a forest, an unkindness of ravens appeared. She had a majesty that made the world permanently yield to her tiny frame. It seemed impossible that she would not forever sparkle, impossible that she would not always love me. A new colour discovered and lost to time. The blossom on a tree that grew once upon a land in a garden never picked. The sweetest fruit swinging singly on a bough, unable to be re-created or sung about.

I'd never have guessed in the days when the lighthouse of her smile guided me gently away from the rocks that I would want to murder a man to keep the ledger balanced correctly in the universe. One could talk of love, but that seems insulting, insulting to call it something so simple, so small, only four letters, something that any child can write on a poster or any yob can scream from the stands. Love was the gloss that caught the light. This was what it felt to have it at first sight.

Tres.

In Catalonia the dogs howl into the muggy evening,
adding to the thickness, conversing in terse tones.
The folk sipping at *Kalimotxo* ignore them. I can hear
Sam calling from high above Paral.lel. It was as clear as
my own mother calling me down for dinner. The German
shepherd directed his barking straight at me and tracked
his snout as I walked. Again and again he repeated the
same thing.

      Asshole, that asshole there, that guy, that guy,
that guy, the asshole.
If anyone else could have understood, I might have been
in trouble. A Pomeranian I did not know, a tourist, cut
her eye at me and flounced past in the opposite direction.
The local quadrupeds muttered to themselves about the
mad German up on the terrace, but a human, a weight

would only be irritated at the ill-disciplined mutt who likely needed walking more. Sam kept insisting that that guy was an asshole. I couldn't argue with him, takes one to know one. Not a pure breed and let me tell you hounds don't see it the way the *weights* see it. It's not lady and the tramp in their world. He was part Rottweiler, part shepherd. He had a huge round head, his looks from his dad. He had issues about that and he didn't mind telling you. A sweet fellow on the whole, but as he beat the streets muzzled by his *weight*, his tourettes accompanied a limp. A low guttural gruffness played on his vocal chords, a rumbling of discontent as if he couldn't bear the city or the hot concrete on his pads without telling it to fuck off as he cleared his throat. He would sit and stretch a yawn. A high pitched yap like an arrow escaping from its string, an action more than likely a simple mechanical linkage from one end of his body to the next. No more than the smoothing of the tired yawns of his muscles and the release of kinetic energy around his gums. The sort of sigh that one affects as they pick up a pencil from the floor, about the time you are the tallest you will be. It is as much about the distance to the ground as the relative years you have spent getting there.

For Sam, it was a giant cock on the toilet door of life. He couldn't yawn or sit without telling no-one in particular, human or dog alike to go fuck themselves.

He had taken his size from his hound father and his hips from his bitch mother. A sad thing to see when a shepherd drags his ass and Sam knew without a shadow, that one day, one day soon, his hind would give out and the ability to hold two fingers up to the rotation of the earth with the arrogance of a child, would give him the slip. No more sitting down and telling the world it was in his pocket. At some point the stick would chase him and he was going to howl, yip, and grumble until that day. I flipped him the bird as I crossed to his side of the street so he could no longer see me.

Dinking off of Para.lel and headed toward Blai, the buildings leaning closer in toward each other, colluding, whispering behind the sheets which hung in front of every terrace. The strip of sunshine thinned, the people changed. A mixture of Spanish, Africans, Arabic folk, the sandstone of ancient, older buildings. With a squint you could step back a hundred years.

Being dragged back in time brought me to her again. The eternal question, why had she left me? Why forever did not last? Would it have made any difference to fate if I had protested at that moment? Watching another man place his lips where yours should be. The stunned disability of your limbs. You might think that you would wrap your bony fingers around the neck of the man who cuckolded you. You have played it out in your mind a hundred times. Every time that a guy scanned your love top to bottom, you wonder at the moment you would massage that face with a knuckle sandwich. Then when it happens, nothing. You laugh at the ridiculousness of it. The killer that exists just below the surface, the temper you had continuously kept in check is actually a toddler. He was better looking than I was. Not that I scaled myself out of tens, but I saw his pretty French face and felt it pulp under the weight of my punches and I laughed.

I walked away. I lost myself in a dream; the nightmare became my waking life. By the time I thought about it closely, it was too late. She was gone, she had left with him and after a thorough year of parties, sex and drugs I heard of her beautiful corpse. I was here in the dry town when I heard. I can't remember which wire I heard it on. It didn't seem to matter. I could imagine her. The blue on her lips as pretty as a sparrow's egg. I heard that she had died in the tub. She had overdosed and slipped below the surface, just enough that the water had entered her lungs. Had she been sober she might have been able to repel its invasive and slippery grasp. Where was the Frenchman, while she bathed? Getting more gak to feed her I'd wager. It's a question I'd like to ask him when we finally meet.

That lance in my mind the energy to keep me driving forward without her. Every nasty word I had ever said to her huddled in a corner with regret, chickens ruffling and keeping each other warm. A zoo of every harsh word spent, hard to remember the sweet parts. An ark of feelings would be nice, one good, one bad up the ramp together they would travel. I had chided her for panicking out in the sea, I had wanted to discuss it and she had shut me down, exasperated by my pushing. A French man had come over because of our arguing, to see if she was ok and that was it. No words were spoken to me, just her rigid body answering the touch of my hand. Once death had beaten its wings so closely, the wash of its cloak, the turbulence in the air snuffed out the flame we both tended. It couldn't let us live. She had to go, she had to move on, death came and instead of taking us out in the ocean, it had killed her love right there on the sand. It drained from her colour. Fell from her as rapidly as fading tan.

Death, a tactile fellow when he/she/it comes, has to feed, has to snack, to lay its bony fingers on some part of the scene. Something has to give, to dry and curl, to crumble between its grip. Chips were cashed, a price had to be paid and that price fluttered on a swing tag pinned to my heart and on another man's head.

Quatre.

At night, the teenagers gathered in the paving below the terrace. I would often look down and watch them. They were beautiful always. They were flawless. I couldn't remember so many girls being so beautiful when I was a boy. If they had been, maybe I would still speak and would have married and divorced them all with the enthusiasm of a kid at the fair. The girls were more giving then I had remembered, when it had been me at that age. Down below in the shadows of the streetlights, a golden brown bunny busied herself with her be-capped, teen heartthrob. Bass notes hummed gently in his pants as the girl let him smooth down her curves and rub her russet dress however he wished. An involuntary touching of the filter tip as I imagined the salt on her lips left from a quick dip at the beach. A thin line of down on her neck and the temperature difference inside her that she would give for a hot word.

I wanted to be that boy, to remove the socks of my experience and throw them in the basket. I wanted to jump from the terrace and sky dive into the soul of that teen. To taste the lashes of that girl and have some comfort. To take her naivety into account. No matter that she would wish of me to speak of love, in exchange for bases. I could do that, nowadays, if I could articulate the vowels and consonants. I could do that. Once you have killed the man inside you, you can do many things, most of all lie for the comfort of love.

So easy to hate when you are young and full of vinegar, easy to drop the word from your lips as a teenager. So much more difficult to love. I could be that boy, could touch that breast for a simple pale word, a white lie. Every scent of sun cream and mosquito oil on the wind brought waves of our holidays to the mind. Out in the darkness of the mountain, the crickets rubbed their thighs wishing to start fires, the noise a solemn texture in the dark.

Her soft breaths seemed to time with my quiet heartbeat, the possibility of a current of honeyed

sweetness on the tides in her eyes and the crest of her
lips toying at the mind. Lost to the recurring dream of
her memory. So real: if I closed my eye lids and placed
my fingers upon them, it was as if thoughts pushed
back against the digits. No honour too high for her,
no softness too gentle, no gas lighter, the earth knew
no baby as valuable, swaddled in folklore, touched by
goddesses and spun into apples. The dew that formed
on her when she was hot could nourish a legion of ants.
Dizzy with her scent they would give up work for the
day and lay siege to the queen in a riot of lustful, six-
legged assaults. The colours she used to tell me she
saw when we had sex still burned brightly. They had
no names; they swirled like aurora around the room,
inexplicable, off the chart, indivisible by red, green and
blue. They were for me and me only. Her aura alight in
the room, the noises she had made, soundless unless they
fell on my ears. She was an exhausted tree in the forest.
If she had keeled over, could anyone hear her crash to
the ground? If her love wasn't there to hear, to see, to
know, until it was too late, did she make a sound?
It was late, the teenagers had gone. Nothing but drunks
howled as the garbage trucks humped treasure to the

seagulls far into the night. Echoing down the hall to the terrace, the elevator engaged, the rollers gear into motion. The hairs on my neck stood to attention, as if a secret knock had been uttered and awaited the long lift hand over fist from below. A heavy thump from the studs of God's briefcase as it stopped on floor three, a swing of the door like a dog chasing hares in its sleep, a shuffle, a scuff and four quick female steps walked down the tiled steps to my door. I could hear her waiting, imagined that she could hear me hearing her and this was why she had stopped. She placed a palm on the door, spread her fingers and tapped softly with her index. I knew it was her index finger, knew the weight of it as it had traced my brow a hundred times.

"What is it that you want?"

"I want in."

"You can have anything, you know that."

"That wasn't always the case. You used to call me a 'Princess,' you weren't always so nice."

"I wasn't a bad guy. Maybe I said something horrible when sometimes I should have said something nice. Maybe I used to think it kept you honest."

"Are you going to open the door?"

"Can we make love?"

"Open the door."

Obediently I turned the handle and swung open the door. There was my next door neighbour foraging for keys in her bag... drunk as a sailor and breathing like a horse. She didn't see me. I closed the door quietly and went back to the large life boat of dreams.

Cinc.

She was a child of revolutionary parents. I affectionately referred to her as, "*The lefty goat stroker.*" Her parents had covered war zones and she had been brought up in the safety of Islington. We had holidayed in the danger zones, off the beaten track. Thailand was no good, it had to be Cambodia. Land mines were preferable to elephant rides, a lawless state where she was a prize to be ransomed better than the purest ecstasy over full moon bay. And she was right; we saw an alien planet that only the language of the Khmer existed within. No cola adverts on billboards or western celebrity gripping the watch they counted time with. The odd white man strayed into our path but for the most part, the country was frozen in its own age. A generation of people wiped out, a strand of experience leapfrogged. Ghosts in every paddy field, adverts in a beautiful script that we could not read. A planet from the future and the past. Tropics dotted with temples thousands of years old. A health and safety babel where local children, tourists and police clambered over stones, roots and rocks for a better vista of the sunset. Cops would sell their badge for a bunch of notes, limbless beggars outnumbered the wildlife. Buddhist monks spoke into cellular phones and children shat in the street. It was a far cry from two weeks in Marbella and so when she told me that she wanted to go to a Tsunami-ravaged Sri Lanka the following year, I simply said, "why not?" She was always right.

She had wanted to surf, I could a little, not the best qualified to teach. Only wanting to have fun, hanging ten was not the point. I rented a janky gun at the only shack and walked it back to her. One other body on the beach, a French man reading Proust and smoking between pages. The leash ran behind him, snagging the sand and alerting the Frenchman to the possibility of a water snake before looking over his sunglasses as if he wanted to extinguish that cigarette in my eye. I reeled in the leash and drew the shape of an armadillo into my mind. The Frenchman had no need to be so unfriendly and

something rattled me that a total stranger had scowled
so. I thought once more of my leathery shelled spirit
animal and resolved myself. It was true his tan and his
library were finer, but clearly from the way he exhaled
his cigarette and propped himself up as if resting on a
plinth in the Louvre, no amount of vitamin D or 18C
literature would soften the nub of a prick growing below
the skin on his forehead. Leaving that one negative
wave behind and walking toward the girl, it was as if my
poles had been left with an excess of electrons by the
Frenchman and the protons of my girl drew me in.

She lay there, aeons away, glowing as if freshly
painted on the sand. The faintest of sweat varnished
her skin. It was impossible to tell if her eyes were open
behind the giant beetle that covered them. As she gained
in mass, my eye trained on her. Not moving my attention
for a moment. She scaled over every imprint I left in
the sand. Her slender tummy we hoped one day would
carry our wonders. One leg cocked up, knee bent ninety
and dusted in crystals. As tasty as a doughnut dropped
in icing. She seemed placed on the *playa* lighter than the
soul of a dragonfly, she was a hinge on which everything
could turn. I felt sure I could draw a line in the sand

and fold it back to view the cosmos… that she could slip her hand into the inky undershoots and pull out the molten heart of a star. She moved her arm unconsciously across her breast, momentarily obscuring the line of her androgyny, her bosom giving her the whisper of a woman where the deaf might see only girls. Only tattoos could make her older. The softness of her skin a coat that would last her for all seasons. The whip-thin line of her frame, a Holly Golightly running barefoot in the park. A fairy. A nymph. A muse. Even now I remember that I wanted to pick her off the sand and cradle into her neck, rock to and fro behind her ear and couch her forehead upon my lips.

I arrived over her and shaded her with the board. A demi-god, Poseidon's son, Mr. California to you. She slid her glasses up and smiled.

"What a dream boat."

We slipped into the shallows, getting the feel of it. Ignorant to the tug at our ankles, a pleasing sensation, little water babies caressing and sweeping us off our feet. Angelic droplets with razor-sharp teeth. Wave after Indian wave crashed all around. Like hawkers at a bazar, noise and colour and beautiful confusion, those Indian

waves and Indian currents swirling us away into the
Indian Ocean with ease.

Sis.

When she stood and looked at herself in the mirror, she felt old. It mattered not how she stood: front, back, port or starboard. Whichever way she adjusted her pose, there was a bit of grey dusted in there somewhere and her hair didn't shine like her eyes still did. They were her best feature, her eyes. Long brown lashes attached to deep pools of chestnut. She had always wanted to have a blue one, just the one. She thought it might make her exotic. Her senses were all there. She'd never had much of a nose, but her eyesight was keen and she could still hold a piss for ten hours straight. She looked at herself a little longer, pulled a few faces and checked her teeth. She sat for a moment and ran through…

who me?

i love you so much.

And her particular favourite.

is that my ball?

She was a looker even pushing forty. She didn't know her exact age and didn't celebrate any kind of birthday, leaving that to pampered pups and celebs.

Her *weight* grabbed the house keys off of the side table. She ran to her. The weight stopped, she sat, the weight held her muzzle firmly.

"Barbara you stay now, be a good girl!"

She exited up the hall and allowed the door to shut, run its own course. Her footsteps, echoing the short distance to the front door, abruptly stopped as the heavy iron and wood casting shut behind her.

Barbara had not heard two *clunks*, only the communal door and so she went to investigate. The door to the apartment was open a crack, resting on the curve of the latch, the heat of the August days expanding the metal by microns and catching it slightly. She could feel the cool hall breeze on her wet nose. Her hackles stood instinctively with interest and she swayed two or three times before standing to attention again, cocking an ear and angling her face so she could point an eyeball to the crack. Nothing.

She waited like that for minutes until she began to hear the soft scuff of the heavily laden Cartero limping his bag down the street. She was excited, her tail swished from side to side as if clearing her desk for the day. She could feel the blood pump of her freedom with every one of his shifted steps. The shadow of the humped delivery man appeared at the mottled glass. He buzzed hopes of entry across multiple buttons, upping his hit rate for admission. An unrecognisable señora voice answered, to which he responded with a cheery, "Correo, entregas!" The door buzzed long and with a caboose loosening click, sunlight spilled onto a cold tiled floor. In one movement she buried her nose in the gap, swung the door outwards and bounded straight at the postman. She gave him a bark, bass-full and throaty to freeze him momentarily and ducked headlong between his thighs, nutmegging him and emerging into glorious sunshine. Her tongue hung sideways as she sprinted like a young whippet out of the gate, disappearing up Diagonal Mar with a full set of lungs and the lights telling her to run.

She had no reason to heed the green, for like all canines she was colour blind. It was pure chance that junction after junction changed for her; maybe the lights envied her spirit. Like Moses parting a red sea of blinkered street furniture, she sprinted onto each go light just as it changed. The wave of repetition catching up to her or vice versa. As a spinning rim moving against the flow of the wheel, the rhythms of the redhead and the red light would funnel into an inescapable destiny. Had she become tired before the lights, her bolt might not have ended so abruptly three yards into the intersection of Carrer Marina where she met *El Abañil Isuzu.*

The builder, winced and complained to the government in the sky at the damage to his beloved van's undercarriage, as he assumed he'd hit another hole in the road.

⊠Y pa esto le doy mi dinero a Madrid?

He squeezed the gear stick into third and she was released from the wheels to the gutter. She lay there heaving, smiling, panting, trying to catch her breath, figuring out what had happened. She slipped in and out of consciousness, but no pain went through her mind.

She kept thinking how old and fat she had felt looking in the mirror and how young and fast she had felt a moment ago. Her life flashed before her seven times faster than the human eye. From the teat to the truck she lay there for nearly ten minutes before a kindly man placed his hand on her ears and stroked them gently. He lifted her jowls and looked at the heavy bleeding from her mouth, told her she was a good girl, such a beautiful girl, that she was "there, there, there, Que buena chica." He spoke to her clearly, the clarity was unnerving, convinced she must be hallucinating, which she probably was, she thought of her *weight* and her favourite line from a mid-afternoon teleplay. "I give you my soul, forever and always, I give you my soul." Her brown eyes darkened, blackened. She died with the taste of the mute's fingers on her lips.

Set.

I did not know her. Beautiful deep red hair, curly and
matted in the impact zone. She was broken. Poor girl.
The life had long gone out of her. She was barely alive
when I saw her, I caught the thinnest wisp before that
was it. A tragedy she had been left here. Unseen, ready
for the horse cart. Probably a tourist, but I had to try
and find out where she was from. I called the municipal
dog pound to pick her up. As they loaded her into the
van, I pedalled my heavy iron-piped bike, the rattling
Harvey Stevenson in the opposite direction, two blocks
in the one way system, then curb hopped the last block.
The four legged morgue. *El gos del mort. El déu del
Dogtown*. The last respect for the nameless four-pawed.

    I waited in the purgatorial room. I have no idea
how long. Beginning to be lost in melancholy. Lost in

the minds of the flies that rubbed their legs together on the walls, scheming for shit. The ink well of the ball point pen being worked slowly in cascading arcs by the secretary. A young boy lay with his head on his father's lap. He had probably already been told that their beloved Fido had been taken to a 'farm'. A woman who could have been his mother but was not, scratched absently at her breast. I lied to myself I wasn't waiting to see a clearer picture of those tits in my cerebral x-ray machine. She looked over briefly but, unsure whether I was eyeing her up through my shades, looked away.

Ideas hung in the air like particles, fragments so tiny, one could breathe them in, ingest them through the tear ducts, taste them in the nasal canal and rub them mixed with sweat. Today was too much to take. They happened sometimes, I get that. I was having a bad day, but a dead comrade, an innocent bitch was too much to take. The lazy rubbing of the woman opposite massaged my head into a trance-like state. Wet hair was being dried by a velvet towel and I could feel it sapping my mind.

I comforted myself that this was why I had chosen this city. It was alive and there was too, too much, to see, to do. It was the only place I had ever been that had turned the eye more than she had. The only place I had been with her where she blended with the texture, the colour and the women. Even the garbage was pretty, picked up by dust deities. The city had so much beauty to give, it was being thrown away. One could push one's fingers into the ancient soul of the town and feel its curses and its blessings, the uneven surfaces that jarred so beautifully with its glass towers, the lights that fell on the corners throwing a sprinkling of magic dust. And yet she had stuck out like a toffee-covered thumb everywhere else we had been... no matter the beauty of the place. In the primordial jungles of Cambodia she had landed in short focus as if fashioned from his Adam's rib, ready to bite into an apple. Among the ghosts of Bokor mountain, the darkest peak in the clouds, she was radiant, a cut diamond jewel you could plunge into and see the refracted self through the light band within. Not here in dry town, simple sleepy Barcelona where she had seemed mortal.

The surface of the city crawled all over by sun-kissed chocolate treats. I am the Easter bunny living the Morpheus of a sorcerer's apprentice. The beauty

extended so generously across the widths of the city that
normally plain calves on a stout German girl seemed
lovelier than a first kiss at midnight. The damn tightness
of each and every knee blurred the lines of ages. If one
watches a girl long enough, she will become a woman. If
you glanced quickly enough at an old woman she would
reclaim her youth. The fantasies of love and certainty
projected onto maids and stewardesses. Give her a
degree, make her a scientist, a farm girl, but make her
twenty one. Make her twenty one until her boyfriends
arrive and their aping and laughing give away her
maturity. Reluctantly, make her a girl again. Be ashamed
of yourself. Be ashamed that you could not see the signs,
until you thought what cannot be unthought.

Everywhere there were hints of her. It cemented
everything I had ever hypothesised of her being one
with the universe. They would find traces of her in dark
matter... perhaps the only part of it which would reflect
light. The colour of the sky on rare occasions conformed
to match her eyes. The pattern on a building intricately
resembling a vintage blouse she could have worn. The
verve of a child to its mother, and the way an old woman
might lazily shoo a mosquito reminded everything in me

of her memory. The good and bad jokes she would tell. And the sun, oh how the sun warmed, burned, caressed every slice of bare skin, made you squint with its intensity and miss it when it was gone. She was in every ray, she nourished and scolded, hid in the corners, shone resplendent and sent mortals cowering for cover. I chose this ancient city, which seemed forever to show its pulse, so that I could never, never, always forget her here.

I am repeating myself, no wonder she left, just an old man who cannot forget and does not remember. She would not look back. It was me that played Persephone, she, Orpheus. Clear eyed views of every step forward, dewy thoughts and misty memories wondering whose they are, ever could be. Under the influence and leading the light, between the sheets, covering up, naked as your birthday, shamed, sullen, stepping out with an inaudible beat. Peeling tones through a foundry of bells sent to the bottom of the heart. A vast cavern, an archive of feelings that had their puppet lines cut long ago.

Vuit.

Bruto lay in the dirt shading his eyes with a paw. It gave him an impression of not caring but I knew he was excited to see me…as if his tail had a brain of its own. The rear half of him swept the dust back and forth. A wiper on intermittent, every step towards him the tail got faster as if the rains came down harder and harder. His paw still did not move from his brow. An English Mastiff with incalculable folds covering his face. Lord of Gracia, the biggest and most feared of all the dogs in the neighbourhood, yet he was a gentle soul. The rightful heir to a district which had been founded by nuns. Sisters of Mercy, thanks, Gracia.

you look like shit bobby.
He always did this. Called me Bobby. I think he called

everyone Bobby, it was mate, geezer, fella to him.

why'd you always call me Bobby?

bobby's a good guy.

I guess so. You know I'm not him.

but what a guy.

Ok how you been?

Just like that? Into the small talk, no epiphany to begin? dazzle me mother fucker. you think it's so interesting to kick dust at my own shit? i'm a basic brit. but you bobby, you're a diamond. always got a story to live, to tell, like you stand in the street on a different corner to everyone else. give my ears a tickle and speak softly bobby. hit me with one of your pearls.

This was his trade off, he always needed a story. Sometimes I told him the same one, with different characters, this time I made up a new one. I did as I was asked. The soft lining of Bruto's ears was magnetic, cartoon gloves could not have been softer, once I had touched every part of them, I gave them a little sniff before kissing them.

There was a place I used to go when I was a child; an old copse, with an ancient ship that had been beached there long ago, I was told... a ship anchored in the ground and unmoved for centuries. Because of this, the ship no longer needed its sails all year around, only in summer. And so every autumn, the wind would shake her vanes and timbers, batter her sails and strip the rigging to the floor before growing it all back in time for spring. What became of this rigging I hear you ask? You don't miss a trick do you?

Bruto's ears perked up with interest.

> Or should i say stick?
>
> what?
>
> Sticks, they fell to sticks.
>
> more than one?
>
> Hundreds.
>
> hundreds and hundreds?
>
> Uh huh.
>
> were you allowed to throw them?

Of course you were, there's nobody else there, the sailors long gone, their rigging for the taking, free to be flung as far as you like.

> heaven.
>
> Yep.

Bruto sat up higher as if something had just occurred to his tiny mind.

that's an amazing story bobby. a real zinger. can I
lick your face?
I looked at Bruto his eyes high in their sockets, his nose
dipped low to the ground, weight shifting from paw
to paw. I loved this part of him, he was a formidable
creature, but when he acted like a pup I loved him dearly.

Yeah ok, gentle huh?

ole, mother fucker.
In the mid afternoon sun Bruto diligently worked his
magic all over my face. He could feel every bump
and ridge, the Braille tongue, children of a lesser dog.
Gently cupping, sucking and licking. It was an enormous
pleasure for him. He read so much into the various
lines and cracks, the length of the stubble excited his
tongue. The lack of soap on my face, washing like
a bum, a dream for Bruto. I knew he could taste the
Mediterranean within the pores and every experience
of life on every epidermal cell. Bruto couldn't read all
the sensations and emotions from his tongue, but he
could taste the sadness that ran to the surface from the
mind and had he been a forensic scientist and, not a
dog, deeper questions would have to be asked after such
a mauling. The level of intimacy between human and

animal showed strangely to the outsider.

A family of Germans found it hilarious until Bruto stopped, dropped his chin to the side and growled low and direct at them. I could have told them to mind their own business, waved them off with a hand or given chase myself, but Bruto loved to be protective. The family paused as they took pictures, Bruto angry that these *weights* felt he and I were a circus and so dropped a bark so full and throaty that the father gripped his children around the scruff and dragged them away. Dripping with saliva and smiles, I watched the Germans scuttle away in haste. Bruto's hackles and the blood that had infused them had now got the better of him and as he went back to his task, he began to mount.

whoa there!

A sharp slap across his wet chops snapped him out of it and he was sitting submissively, head cowered, eyes in the tops of his sockets, asking for forgiveness.

it happens. sorry. not that i see you that way but it's pretty hard for me to get ass you know. sends you a little crazy at times and the head can get confused with the balls. sorry.

It's fine.

you sure?

Yeah really, but put the lipstick away will you.

lipstick?

I nosed a motion at his belly.

no, no, no that's not connected.

Bruto sat with his legs under him in and waited for the pinkness to subside. He did not know who the redhead was, but said he'd keep his nose to the wind and his ears to the ground.

Nou.

"Assolir la pilota, buscar la pilota de merda..."
The children chasing a ball below woke me. The type
of awakening that opens your eyes for you and in that
millisecond you realise you are alive again. Nothing like
the usual alarms, neither the neighbour's dog, a doorbell,
or a good dream slowly leading you from the woods into
the light. My eyes opened with the force of a rat trap
spring. I popped into consciousness, like a beer bottle
that is either sealed or open. There is no real in-between.
That was this morning. I would not have minded being
dragged half-awake into another reality, slowly finding
one's feet somewhere other than the sands of time I have
been sleeping through. It was not that on this morning.
I was dead to the world, defibrillated and then *snap!*
My eyes and mind opened as one. A carbonated crown,

wrenched from the lips. I felt almost reborn. Breaking the surface tension of a holy pool and dragged into the air to breath by an invisible priest. Hair matted and wet with perspiration, the heat of the afternoon arrived early to the morn, like waking inside a tea bag recently pulled from the cup.

There on the pillow next to me, the one I never used, the placing set for a mystery diner, a single red hair burned and highlighted by the sunshine. Through the cracks of the *persianas* framed by the slats of light, it sat up praying mantis-style and begged her to be remembered. I left it there to guard the cotton and padded to the kitchen to stoke the pot. Not enough grounds to fill the stoker, it lay at half weight reminding me of a shallow grave. Screwed it shut, lit the gas and lay on the floor of the kitchen to wait. The cool stone on a saline encrusted back was comforting. An incandescent flicker of the strobe racing the electricity through me, my eyes, even closed, conducting a charge. Hairs the length of my arms raised like the dead of a long-forgotten cemetery. The atmosphere in the apartment was thicker than I could ever remember. The unmistakable fog of two people's pheromones. The hair on the pillow meant nothing. It was the air between each spark of light above and my back laying on the floor earthing and anchoring the energy flow. It wasn't love, unsure even if it was lust, but it was real. Slices of lucidity falling through my mind like slides in a gate, our grand and silent exercise broke through as clear as sun through the blinds. Something had come loose. A vigorous fuck had left bearings and screws misplaced and rattling in the pit of my stomach. Where they had fallen from I could not yet tell. The pot burst into life and gargled more pleasantly than a cockerel might wake me from my slumber. Care and attention followed the roll onto all fours, rocking back and forth on hands and knees, discs and vertebrae fell into place like well-drilled cadets. Laying on all fours prone. Fucked in the ass by the morning reality. A one night stand, I sat up straight and threw myself onto a cocked knee that pushed in opposition to my other foot. Head up, clean and jerk, to step forward with a flat back, file from drawer.

Cold lipped and drunk as a barrel, I remember that much about her. Her hair seemed to light the street as we walked home. She was much too much of a woman for me. It was surprising that she took notice. Heels that sat so snugly on her pretty feet, she could have passed for a satyr. The recently slicked paving wet down, giving us the impression of a storm we had missed while drinking. She had lost someone, she didn't tell me who, it didn't matter. The lights hanging directly overhead the middle of the street, dropping a halo of light in front of us every sixteen drunken steps. A reminder that angels existed.

She might have filled that spot, but she had a furrow of evil running through her, she was a composite, not pure, there was a sandwich layer that made her stronger, gave her the spine she needed to be a nasty bitch without it affecting the other materials. She gave you the impression there had been a version 1.0 redhead. And that one hadn't faired so well. It had suffered from the reality of life and its cruelties, so this one had been built stronger, with a take no prisoners and give no mercy doctrine impregnating her. If I had to guess and I was doing nothing other than that. She hadn't said much to me and I had said exactly zero to her with my lips. At least there was nothing that made noise from them. I could do a lot with a smile, a furrowed brow and a wrinkled eyebrow or two. More than you would

think. With practise you can say so much with just the
eyes. So I told her quite a bit, but in the end from what
I remember, she didn't want to talk. She had the feel
of a woman lit up by a guy like me. Strong, silent, able
to fuck her without the need to discuss contraception.
She wanted it rough, yet with a comforting nuzzle to
accompany each plunging stroke. She wanted something
that she had never got from whomever had broken that
pretty heart.

     I was drunk, so, so drunk, but I remember thinking
that sometime not so very long ago, she would have
been a sweet girl with a heart untraded. Long ago I
might have missed the girl she no longer resembled. I
might have wished for a flash of the woman that I could
smell at the corners of her, but not now. It piqued me,
sat up and told me of its truth, but I was glad not to have
an overripe *chica*, too easily bruised to deal with and
I think she was glad to bang her sturdy husk against
another hive-minded individual. I do not know when she
left. At some point our tanks became empty and sleep
overwhelmed me. We did not spoon, there was no need
in such night heat. She pushed me away once we had
known one another several times and there I stayed until

I awoke. Were it not for that hair, I could have forgotten her entirely, convinced myself she was figmentum. I still could, the inner voice scratched at me, but I didn't.

Deu.

I had to let her go. Had to, you understand. There were no other choices. Each white wave pummelled the muscles I held on with. We were being washed out. I had to paddle with both arms and then a wave broke us apart. And I let her go. I wanted to live and I was going to die if I held onto her surfboard. She was leashed onto the board by her wrist, I had secured her but she didn't want me to let go. With the tightest of times and jaw lines, I screamed for her not to panic, pressed firm on the Velcro and told her she had to hold on to the rails. She needed me to stay with her, she screamed for me not to leave her. It rattled my soul at that moment, I knew that I could do nothing else and yet it was wrong of me. As if our lives had led to this point and I had let go at the only moment she needed me not to.

She saw me leaving her, not just letting go. It didn't matter that it was the right thing to do, the safe thing to do, the smart thing to do. I still let go and she saw it. I saw her question my love for her then in that moment. Her face read that all was lost, the world had ended, her foundations broken. We tumbled in the break, caught and lost inside until I surfaced and she was still lying on the board. Still screaming for me not to leave her. A wave started to take her forward. I shouted ''GO!'' She paddled as the lip of a foaming colt began to carry her towards shore and I set off with leaden arms stroking after her. We traversed sideways through the rips and began to gain some ground on the surf. Some ground.

Onze.

The way the wolf tells the story is the truth, so he says.

He says the way the bear tells the story is different. If the bear tells the story she finishes it with you.

You're better off hearing it from me.

Dotze.

Bruto walked next to me and mumbled under his breath
as he nosed each lamppost. I stopped each time he
stopped, it was a slow walk. He read the crease between
the wall and the street in perfect olfactory fluency.
We were walking not too far behind a young girl and
her Husky. Not too far, quickly became a long way
which seemed a shame because she was beautiful and
her Husky was female. We might have double-dated
had Bruto not been such a slowcoach. I thought about
pointing out the cute Husky to him, but figured he would
have smelt her long before I saw them and if he had
wanted to chat her up, he would have done so. Bruto was
not the sort to let an exotic creature from the north get
away, if it interested him.

     shit sparky, haven't seen him for a while. judy fly

jordi corky sam mmhmm all them usuals.

He plodded on.

jota bay alessio perro sam ...

He stopped, sniffed again with more care.

sam

He repeated.

i do not like that fuck.

He shifted sideways and cocked a leg, looking back at me, he plopped his tongue out and blinked both eyes. It was his way of winking, I felt at a loss of being unable to piss in the street without being arrested and sticking two fingers up in the same salty fashion to those he disliked. Bruto's lofty hind leg kicked out the last drops, each with a vicious grunt. Each leaving the curled-over fur that covered his lipstick cock like punctuation being nailed on a blackboard by an over-enthusiastic, Lit teacher.

Take

That

Fucking

Pussy.

Bruto liked cats, that is to say he had no real problem with them. He would describe himself as the type of hound who "knows a lot of cats, some of my best friends are cats". It did not stop him however from using the feline name as ultimate disrespect.

Sam the cross?

yeah you know him?

A little.

real negative mother fucker. never stops moaning. no wonder he has no friends.

Bruto sat down on the kerb and began to scratch away at his neck, fur fell in huge chunks all around him. He stopped scratching and looked down at the clumps that swirled in a hairy tornado at his feet.

I was naturally concerned for him, but he just shifted the weight on his ass and carried on with the scratch. As each clump of hair fell, it was as if holes appeared in him. Each scratch taking a deeper thing than follicles away. The expression on his face read the same as with every other moment I had witnessed him scratching, utter pleasure. He had found the string that ran him from nose to tail and each stroke of his claws was a chord change like running your fingers down the ribs of a bass string. Witnessing a *dogasm*. I wanted to stop him pulling out his hair but it caused him so much

pleasure the mouth was not able to override the heart.
Let the dying man smoke his cigarettes.

Bruto we can talk later, I need to be getting on.
See you tomorrow?

as you wish bob.

He placed his snout onto his rump, rolled his jowls back
and chewed at the skin there making it a little red.

Fleas?

He flashed me a look that lasted all of a second and had
an air of being insulted about it.

See you.

He did not reply, but continued to chase his ass around
looking for that itch.

Tretze.

She had been bookish, solitary and had sat in a corner, worlds away from other children. The moment she could comprehend the words she read, the pages fluttered in her hands as relentlessly as breaths. Each stanza, each scene she laid her eyes on was partly hers. She claimed it, the way a treasure hunter staked gold. Each story belonged to the great library in her mind that would be inherited by no one and would die with her. It saddened her that all this writing could not be shared. She wanted to pass on something that rested deep inside her, something of her own. In the same way that she grabbed the thoughts of others with both hands, she wanted her words to be pawed at by strangers, her books to go into the minds of others, to rest in their inner library, to sit on the shelves of their cities, to ride their town buses and to nestle in the baskets of girls riding bikes. She wanted to be read by pretty dilettantes who sat demurely in the park, pored over by the edgy girls who'd service a man for kicks round the back of a bar. She wanted to be read by the housewives dulled by their square lives... who had nothing until they opened her covers and lived through her pages. She wanted to be read by the professors who would call it out for shit, but secretly love it like they loved their own dicks. She wanted to be read, she yearned to be read.

Feverishly assaulting libraries through college and university without an ounce of real time on operation, she acquired top marks, added many skills and theorised a whole lot with her book club. She poked holes where they should be, scratched posts that looked itchy and made it through a first class Oxford Literature degree without a moment of pleasure that she had not engineered herself. She was schooled, scripted, moulded and set in the right way. What did she have to write about that wasn't something she had read? She could tell you how the rough hand of a lumberjack and a cold night felt on your skin, yet she hadn't felt it, smelt it, lived it or given that lumberjack a pet name of her own. She tried to justify to herself that she had a view, tried to work her corner hard and see the angle that was unique to her, but lacked the conviction in even that. Drastic action might save her and she prayed nightly that something drastic would happen, would jolt her, would send her a sign. She kept her eyes peeled and noted anything that had a pattern, habits, regular occurrences, moments in the everyday and waited for an electric charge. Her shutter perpetually set to bulb, she sat waiting to be exposed, lightning on her back plate.

Then something changed. Dark misfortune befell her. Grief jump-started her heart. Her parents died on holiday, washed away. She hardly knew them. It wasn't a surprise to her. She had always felt like they should have been washed away; a fitting end to an uncomfortable relationship. She had boarded since she was five, her parents had sent her to camps for holidays, she was allowed home for Christmas. She felt as if she were a stain to them. Her mother would rub her hands when she spoke to her as if the girl were covered in grime, as if she were talking to the bin man, the gardener or the local mechanic. As parents, they never discussed her, there were no photos of her on the walls, mantles or in their attic. Was she a mistake she wondered? As if she had been placed in the wrong receptacle by a scatter-brained stork. The milkman delivering her to the wrong house. She was an experiment in procreation that had gone wrong. Her father had thrust when he should have parried. She was the sort of child that was seen and not heard. She was encouraged to be so. Quietly she visited the place where they had died.

In Sri Lanka, Thailand, Aceh they were desperate for help. She took one look at the sea where they had disappeared, thanked them for the money they had left her and began volunteering for a tsunami charity. When they died, she finally began to live. Their deaths opened doors to her that she never knew existed. Her virtual world became a reality. The people, the characters of whom she had read stood in front of her. The tragedies, the ghosts, the beaches, shattered lives, broken bricks and bureaucrats connected in front of her and she wrote it all down. She had no idea where they would all go, but she couldn't help but be pleased that she was finally touching a real life and that she would one day tell others about it.

She began her first relationship. He was a

fisherman in the village. A tragic, lonely man who had lost his entire family while he had been visiting the temple high on the hill.

Kasun had lost a wife, three girls, his boat and his faith. He had only known one woman. His wife Thamalini had been his love since they were children. When Kasun made love to the redhead it was with grief, searching and yearning. He was looking through the ruins of her with each thrust, trying desperately to find the woman he had always known in the avatar of this white girl. Every time he was ashamed of himself. Each time the redhead felt it. She felt his shame make her stronger; she knew that every moment he spent inside her, left another little piece of him behind. Everything he gave to her was magnified as if they were sun and lens. The grief and sadness that he poured into her was concrete, it strengthened her foundations, gave her colour and coldness. His rough callused hands read her all over. Looking for the woman whom he had lost. Looking for the life that had been splintered like matchsticks and rinsed so thoroughly from the planet. They did not kiss; she had wondered if he knew how. It was an exotic experience for her; she felt his sadness, but she felt like a liquidator laying claim to another man's hard graft. Buying up the remains of his broken life and repurposing it for use in another region. She was a sponge, a succubus to his experiences. It excited her to know there would be others. As she wrapped her legs around Kasun inviting him to pour his loss into her, wringing him of the past, never minding that he spoke Tamil to her, rained shameful tears onto her to sate his broken and lustful engine. Each drop hit her chest and evaporated like steam onto the hot bonnet of a desert drag racer. She felt little guilt, even if she knew that in the long run, Kasun was doing himself no good. She knew that the villagers looked at her as though she were a white witch, a whore. The surviving elders made no difference to her. He was whispered about, mocked by his community. It made no marks on her mind. It was his choice, she was giving him a place to be, a place to purge his soul, to scratch in the dirt and claw at the dead within him, hoping to find a semblance of life between their two sets of atoms before the darkness enveloped him fully. Maybe she was a witch, the idea of burning on a stake held no fear for her and this was just one man, this was just one experience and it whet her lips as a babe's first spoonful of solids. She was getting fatter, soon the writer inside her would begin to toddle.

Catorze.

She walked in the fresh sand. The sky was broody and
overcast. Layer upon layer of cloud hid faces in the
folds, smoking demons wrapped in down duvets. The
bricks from the washed away houses still dotted the
coastline like land mines. The beach looked sadder than
usual and the trees that had survived the great waves
hung low like spiders, waiting to catch the wind in their
web. The south Indian breeze ran hard in starts, kicking
the spray off of seven foot white caps that the young
boys rode in the distance. Rooks skimming the surface of
the tourists at the tower, the boys glinted in the sun like
black pearls. They rode patchwork sticks with no leash
and no suit. Fearless and light, they carved the waves.
They bounced in and out of barrels and were gone before
the relentless foam could snap at their heels. She found

a single set of towels lying in the sand, two books, a box of western cigarettes and a bottle of water buried from the sun. The residents of that spot were nowhere to be seen; she scanned the long thin beach.

Further down the sand a few hundred yards or more, a crowd had gathered. Half a dozen people stared at the ground. Something was wrong in that pack and she set off at a jog that turned sprint within paces. She pushed her way past the Sinhalese whose heads were bowed in submission to the gods. A pretty jewel in the shape of a girl lay on the sand. A handsome, tanned, tourist desperately performed CPR on her. She was fascinated in the rhythm and the change between his hands her chest, his lips and her mouth. The beads on his wrist which could have been bought in any market in Asia clacked together as he counted out each hopeful cardiac massage in French. She could tell that this man did not know the prostrate girl; that his performance was purely for the hope, for the chance to grasp the human life that was slowly slipping away. There was no love in his eyes for this girl, only desperation that she should breathe one more time, then a second and a third until she coughed up the water that saturated her lungs and bloated her. His lips to hers were mechanical. He listened one more time to her naked chest before hitting her there harder than seemed necessary. The first aid stopped and he caressed her eyelids, pulling down the shades to the windows and giving up. She saw through the gaps of the locals praying, a man walking away in the distance, sun burnt, slumped shoulders, shaking his head. He was the only other white man on the beach, he became smaller and smaller. It was strange to see a white man walking away from a dead white girl. Strange in this part of the world where the Caucasian faces noted each other in the tens.

A day later she heard rumours about the dead girl. She was English, she was American, she was Swedish. Nobody could nail her nationality to the vine. She decided on a whim and a blankness of her notebook to get involved and went to the local police station, claiming to have had drinks with the girl the night before and likely being the last to have seen her alive before the morning accident. Did she know her nationality?

No.

Would she help with the identification of the body?

She was in the back of the police station looking into the deep freeze at the girl within ten minutes. Yes, that was her, she had drunk no more than three beers, no, there was no one else with her. Had they asked at all the local guest houses?

They were doing so currently.

Did she have a boyfriend with her that night? A husband?

She pointed out that the girl wore no wedding ring on her left hand. The policeman nodded.

Yes of course, a tradition.

He told his assistant to note that down on the report. She was sorry she could not have been more helpful, but to let her know if she could help further.

As she padded down the beach and looked out to shore she wished she had not become involved. The girl had been beautiful, even in a bloated and pale state. Even though her eyes had been forcibly shut, she could feel them staring at her from under those lids and they wondered what business it was of hers. She did not want to help, she was just nosing, she was just experiencing for the sake of boredom. It occurred to her that this is how her parents had laid... on a slab, unclaimed for days.

She felt a grain of guilt for the first time since she had
left Britain and she cast her mind back to the moment
she had seen the crowd on the beach. The man who
had walked away. It wasn't right, but she had no face
to place him with. She had no reason to mention this to
the police, yet she knew she had to find him, to quell her
curiosity.

On her way to the country she had read many facts
about the nation, the perpetual state of war, always on
the fringes of the media, but conveniently ignored by the
West, the cocktail of diseases one could contract in such
a small country, the road deaths, averaging two hundred
per year and the drowned. She remembered the drowned
most of all. Fears of heights and depths came to her in
equal measure. There was no distinction for her to look
up at the mast of a boat or over the side of a building.
The same dizzy plummeting sensation came to her brow.
While floating in the pool, the ocean or the lake when
she could not see the bottom, she felt she would fall,
be sucked into the vortex forever falling, have the life
squeezed out of her by an invisible hand larger than her
body. As if she were a dispensable clay figure that could
be crushed and mixed with the water, dissolved never

to be found. She remembered that hundreds of tourists a year met their fate this way. They came for honeymoons and were swept away with the tide. They had the feet knocked from under them, banged heads on rocks, were tumbled by the force of the waves and brought still by the rips. Such danger in paradise, as if the country were given its immense beauty at a price.

A sacrifice,

A lamb to the gods,

Booby traps on the fringes of Eden.

Never was there a paradise untouched. Beaches without people were so beautiful, private and remote. No one to hear you scream, no one to save you, no one to help, no one to hold your hand. We all die alone, but some of us bear witness to the death of others and she wanted to find out what made a Western man walk away from a beautiful girl laying soaked on the beach. She had found her story, her mystery, her novel. She would find the girl a home, a name, a lover, a resting spot. She would find the man a face, a moral and a reason. Maybe he was nothing. Maybe he was blind. Maybe he was a survivor of the tsunami, exhausted with the death all around. She'd heard the local people didn't sleep near the beach any more. Too many fears, ghosts, memories. Maybe it was like this with him. She tied back her thick red hair as if this helped her make up her mind and rolled the dice of her thoughts before starting at the guest house closest to the beach. She sniffed out a few likely looking twenty-somethings and sat down to chat. No-one at the Happy Cat knew the girl, but they had all heard the story. She left before the owner got suspicious of the intrusion and wondered to herself why she was doing the same thing the police had done. A real dick wouldn't follow the flat foots. A real dick would find her own groove.

She remembered the two beach towels and went back to the sand to hunt.

Quinze.

He moved slowly, his fur seemed to reach out and claw at the breeze to pull him along. He was not well. It's amazing how quickly a dog becomes old. Seven times quicker than you and I. I'm not sure he read the sadness in my eyes, but he felt my heart stir from a hundred paces and he knew when I was coming before I did. His body might have been slipping over the cliff but the foundations of his senses, his soul and whatever animal energy root him in that kingdom were still sharp as flint.

We call ourselves animals, but we're not. We're too bound up in thinking to hear what makes us an animal. It has been reported that dogs will sit by the door the moment their owner gets in the car to leave work. How they sense the impending arrival of their owner nobody knows. At least nobody in the biped world can explain it to each other. The animal kingdom has no need for an explanation, they have no word for trust, it does not exist in their world. That's what asses and noses are for.

How are you?

peachy as a pig in a plum tree.

I'm not sure what that means. It sounds positive though. Are you being sarcastic?

no, its the truth, since my weight found out I was gonna do the long siesta under the porch, he's been treating me like a royal king. keeps filling my bowl up to the top. not that I can eat it mind.

I'm so sorry Bruto. How long have you got?

oh all night, he's drunk and asleep on the sofa.

I was unsure if he deliberately swerved me, but decided I was being insensitive to pursue such a terminal line of questioning. I wondered whether he had seen any of the other fellas since he was diagnosed. It was doubtful for he wouldn't have shown weakness willingly at the park. Why we were meeting in the dark was my first thought. Bruto mentioned his eyes hurt too much in the sun, 'meds' he said. We were hiding his highness's illness it was clear. Like Cromwell and Henry, meeting in secret.

i sent out word about your redhead. nobody knows and when nobody knows something is fishy.

Could just be a tourist no?

we ain't like you lot. there is always someone whose nose has come across them and they haven't, which means she don't exist. nada chico.

That makes no sense at all. I carried her to the ambulance.

i don't want to doubt you bobs, but I sent horatio to look at the junction you say you found her. he didn't smell a thing. i'm sorry guapo.

Oh fucking great I'm having a conversation with a dog who is telling me I'm crazy.

i know right!

Cabron Bruto!!

hey take it easy. don't shoot the messenger. i know i'm dying but let me get a little further up the road before you give me a mercy bullet.

And you. Are you fucking real?

i could still sink my teeth into your ass if you wish.

He pulled his jowls back and growled. It was not

designed to scare me, rather to make me laugh. I didn't feel like laughing. What the fuck had happened that day? She got to me that pup. I haven't stopped thinking about her, feeling about her. I remember the blood stains on her golden coat. I remember her smell, that of an old dog. The smell of water-logged rhododendrons hung around her, the clumps of matted hair around her ears that had not been clipped back. I could tell she dragged them in her food, I remembered thinking it. You don't get that from smoking too much pot. I can't even recall when I last smoked pot. The red dog meant something to me, to a buried part of my mind that I was either refusing to acknowledge or was making up this stuff as it went along.

The Frenchman seemed to be on the fringes of this, it was easy to blame him at this stage. He had let slip the only creature worth living for and I could blame him for a dropped cup of coffee if I wanted. My mother used to think about her best friend who had died tragically young. Every time her shoe laces became untied, she used to like to think that Sue was fucking with her, teasing her and making sure she didn't forget her. The Frenchman was not making sure I did not forget him.

I was making sure I didn't forget him. You don't forget when you see the lips, those you've branded with passion to your own, being kissed by another. You don't forget the one who cuckolds you unless you want to. I don't want to.

He presented himself in adverts for travel agencies, in the looks of lascivious bar men to the pretty English gap year students. He was the asshole who swayed this-a-way and that-a-way, leaning ever closer to puking on you even if you zigzagged around him. The spark of the train that startled you as it pulls into the platform, the annoyance of the jets that broke the serenity of a perfect sky, a hole in my socks, not having enough milk in the fridge to top up a morning coffee: all of these things I attributed to him. All of these things were him reminding me not to forget.

He was Bin Laden.

It was his fault.

He should be hunted, chased, punished.

This administration will not rest until he is captured and killed. Fuck the redhead. Focus! I kept telling myself. The corners of reality were crumbling and no scaffolding could hold it up. I felt as if I were being gentrified without my permission. Developers were taking the character and the brickwork that has stood for so long and knocking it down. They were waving away any protests I made and in answer erecting steel and glass in its place. My subconscious bleating on about sustainability as convincing as the holocaust selling regeneration.

With every step I took down the street with Bruto, I thought of the redheaded woman. I was getting a little stiff in my shorts and at forty five years of age I was glad to still have the blood circulate there. So close to anger is lust. One minute you want to kill a man, the next you want to fuck a girl. Such are the cornerstones of being a healthy red-blooded man. I felt better at the twinning.

Buddy, want to go swimming?

i dont think i can paddle. i don't have the energy. i'll come with you though, no sense in letting you have all the fun on your own.

Setze.

The beach was dotted with fires. The plastic and tin
bottles that were underfoot numbered in the same
column as the grains of sand. Pickpockets worked the
strip as the tourists disrobed and went into the calm
water to skinny dip. It never fazed me to come here on
my own but with Bruto able to watch my back and my
threads, I'd be able to float with the current and let my
worries ripple away in the dark. Bruto and I found a spot
near the big hotel and I folded my pieces in front of him.

    You ok with looking after my stuff while I dip?

    yep.

He placed his jaw over the pile of clothes as a makeshift
pillow, you'd have to be an idiot to try and take them
from him.

    Show me your angry face.

He pulled back enough flesh around his snout for his
considerable fangs to catch the moonlight.

Do the noise.

He grumbled so softly it made me want to cuddle him,
but would make a street walker run a mile.

Change tone.

He let loose a deep bark like wood block snapping at a
black board.

You the man.

no you the man, i'm the faithful hound.

He dropped his face again and lifted each eyebrow
one after the other in semaphore. If he weren't my best
friend, I'd want him to be my dog and me to be his
weight, without a shadow of doubt.

The sea chilled my feet, there was no surf.
Stepping into a glass of water with big boots, the line
of temperature worked quickly with each sunken pace
through the sand. As the ripple moved from the ankles
upwards I felt half full. It was here that I missed her
most. It was here that I loved her last, it was always here
that I try to wash her from me.

Disset.

A sea of letters crashed over us again and again. The type huge, too impossible to read for its size. The collective number of letters in the alphabet seemingly more than the twenty six I was used to using. As if the various alphabets from east to west had banded together and held arms like riot police at a picket line.

News print.

A story.

Obituaries.

The pressure crushing the life out of my chest. A hundred articles rained down on me. I could see how our deaths were reported in copy big and small. Sometimes an inch no more. Other rags defied the logic of a couple of western bodies lost to a country that lost thousands a year and printed pictures with the obits. Most were unsuccessful in capturing the spirit with which we had been caught out. None managed to wrap the love *the tourists* felt for each other into a satisfactory paragraph. The fact that she would be described in red tops as a brunette, slight and pretty and that I was described as carrying seven years her senior didn't bother me. It bothered me that I was reading obits at all. As each fist of fonts weighed us down, the pages of our collective history curled over us like dog-eared, salty broadsheets.

Our final breaths about to be reduced to a page number and sold for pennies in the pound. I would not let it happen, then I saw her take a mouthful of foam as she screamed for me not to let go. This is the moment you realise you are not Superman. It broke my spirit just then to know that the last thing I did was let her down. My last memory of her to be the one where I could do nothing. I had always told her, promised her with hand on heart, that I would do anything for her. I would never let her down. She was the best thing that had ever happened to me and I would sell my right arm if it meant she could have three. In the end that meant nothing. Impotence just when she needed a strong right hand. The power I had always felt just knowing I was her man, an illusion, useless fucking poetry. Whatever tiny strength there was deep inside meant nothing to the violent majesty of the swell.

A speck in the ocean. Krill being swallowed by a blue whale. We were a nature programme, the audience looked on at the baby gazelle mauled to death and shook their heads at the shame of it before putting on the kettle. She screamed my name and it was lost to the howl of water as it took me down below the surface, all happening in the slowest of moments. So slow we should be dancing together not dying. I launched at her, desperate to try once more and connect. To hold her hand, hopeful that might make some difference. She was continuously swept just out of my grasp. Looking back now, I wished I'd cried. I yelled for her to paddle rather than scream. I could not touch her, my words exhausting me and reaching out invisible to grasp her back. I could feel the grip of her tiny hands in my mind. The white clean nails, rinsed through with salty water. The warmth from her lips was still there. She was still there. Smaller and smaller she became. Different rips taking us from one another. I stroked after her, arms like jelly, no longer sure there was progress. The numbness began in each fibre of my body. A deity readying me for the final curtain. Another mouthful of salt made me vomit the hull of my stomach lining as I tried in vain to grapple with the beast of death. A moment of clarity came from the exhaustion that had beaten me. I lay back for a moment, conserving energy. The Rolodex of memories flickered more slowly as I tried to keep my head above water and steady my creaking heartbeat.

How she held my hand throughout a movie.

Where my face fit perfectly into the space between her shoulder blades.

The smell of her on the towels rather than the smell of the towels on her.

The way she danced with a mixture of excitement and embarrassment.

I could no longer see our spot on the beach. We had been washed around the headland and there was not a boat in sight. I was truly alone, I wanted to find her, I did not want to die alone, only with her. Suddenly I entered the wash of yet another rip taking me further from the course of safety and there was the surfboard's nose sticking from the water. It dragged heavily on its tail to sit straight up, tomb-stoning in the deep water.

Welling up, unable to see straight, I clawed as hard as I could towards the vertical gun. Once I reached a couple of yards from it, I dived. The water calm beneath the surface, such different worlds, the illusion of safety in the quiet. There she was waiting for me. Her mouth open, her eyes fixed, staring into a distance she would never calculate. I swam to her, held her. Late to meet her, late to save her, too late to die with her. Held her tight. We bobbed below the surface for a moment before I kicked and broke the surface tension.

Divuit.

Ana.

Who is it? She asked.

"Ana." He repeated.

Again she asked who it was. Where was she? He
wondered. He had no concern for his own geography,
only in relation to her. If he did not know where he was,
then it was likely she did not know where she was. If
she didn't know who he was, then she could be hurt,
she might have taken a knock to the head. She could be
delirious.

"Ana it's me." He finally slurred.

"Who is me?"

She whispered quietly into his ear. She was close, he
could feel her breath. Her voice continued to move
around.

"Do you know or don't you?"

Was she toying with him? Why was she making this purgatory harder for the two of them? What was her purpose?

Yes.

He answered simply. He said nothing more. Some time passed, how long he had no idea. If it were indeed purgatory then it could have been an age of man. It could have been a weather cycle, the orbit of a single moon or the generation of a grandfather.

He could wait.

He could see out the time. Wait until it became light. Once more he wondered if he had died. It was probably for the best. He had let go of her on that board and she had had to save herself. He could have done nothing for her. He could have at least died for her. That would have shown her the volume and greatness of his love. That would have made her stay. If he had died for her, she couldn't have left. Maybe he had died, maybe they had both died. Again he wondered, his mind fell from one ledge to the next. No racing, simply rolling and lolling as he wondered where he was, where she was. He broke the silence.

"Ana, my soul."

He whispered. Quietly he breathed and could hear the wind rattle through his teeth, his own breath. He inhaled a sigh, it should have gone in the other direction. It came from the depth of his boots and finally she spoke again.

"Tell me who it is. *Me* is not an answer."

This seemed reasonable. He would not trust anyone in this state either. Should he even trust that it was her, that it was Ana? He thought hard about whether he should trust anything. He could still see nothing. He could tell that his eyelids were open, he could tell that it was not dark. It was not, in fact, light either. It was as if his eyes were missing... as if the synapses that signalled shape and colour and focus had missed their junction points. There were no stations left. Information shuttled uselessly along tram lines. The rolling stock had no doors, no space for cargo or passengers. There were no platforms to stop at. There was simply no vision, as if it had been erased from memory.

"Who is this?"

He repeated the question to himself. She wants to know who I am. She wants to know that she can trust her own vision. Maybe she can see me, but she cannot trust that

it is truly me in this place. He pondered the stopgap in
reality. He wondered about her hallucinations. What
he must look like. A horror story, no doubt. No eyes.
Black pits where blue once gazed upon her with such
reverence. As if he might have blinded himself with
some terrible truth. He thought deeply on this for a
moment before his cheek seared red with pain. He had
heard the slap but he did not feel the jolt that should
have accompanied it. Lightning without thunder. A clap
and pain without the movement that comes when the
electrons smash into the positively charged earth. Again
he heard her say more clearly, more force in her voice.

"Who are you?"

There was only one answer for her. He tried everything
else, but the truth seemed like the only option left to him.
The cul-de-sac he found himself in that had no name and
so he told her so.

"I don't know."

He said plainly. He heard the articulation begin to return
to his voice. Her slapping him had at least loosened his
tongue in one sense.

"I don't know who I am."

He repeated. He knew it was the truth. He realised at that

point he had measured himself by what he did know and had ignored what he did not. Like a man who realises the earth is most likely not flat, but has no inclination to explore it. No interest in sailing towards the edge of the world, not for fear of falling off but simply with the disinterest that comes with having known and lost. With the loss of himself went the loss of wonder. It seemed so clear to him at that point, so clear to him that he began to laugh. Long uncontrollable peals only punctuated by coughing spells. She placed her hands on his cheeks. He finally settled and stopped his hysterical convulsions. He could feel her hands holding him. He could feel the tears from his laughter running down his cheeks. She gently licked the tears from his face. It was not something she had done to him before. Heaven had changed them both he thought to himself. Heaven had made her more tactile, sillier, tastier. She slipped her tongue gently into his mouth and he took great comfort at the warmth she placed there. She closed her lips and eased her tongue out from his mouth.

"I love you."

She whispered with confidence. She had never said it like that. He felt a tiny pinch in his neck and repeated her words to himself over and over. He knew that she would be safe. That she was in charge, for a change. He was simply sitting in the passenger seat on this ride. It was a relief to him that she was finally taking over. She loved him. It was good. He was sick of saying it first, sick of teasing it from her by saying it so she replied. A weight lifted from his mind and he slipped gently into the current of unconsciousness, into a darker, colder place that he could ever have imagined.

100

Dinou.

The late evening sun arced and placed itself through the crack in the *persianas*. One missing slat slicing across the lashes acting as one's own blinds, a searing alarm clock. The stripe of heat falling across the pillow's eyeline depending on the time of year. A terrible, heavy head. I could not lift it, I was sure. Didn't even want to try. My mind would not settle. A child had emptied a bucket of Lego onto the floor of my memory and somewhere in there was just one building brick that I needed to find. I could only imagine mountains of colour to sift through with nowhere to start.

The buzzer sounded. I looked over the balcony. It was Bruto. He didn't even look up, he just sat there like a boss. I grabbed a sweater around me, it was getting late into the summer and the nights had a lingering air of both heat and chill depending on your physical activity. Whilst a brisk walk would send you instantly into a sweat, a ten minute chat on the mountain could turn brass.

Tercero

Segundo

Primero

'Sup dog?

sup weight?

I'm not your weight, come on, where we going? I like that you surprised me with a visit.

up the mountain.

Can you make it up the mountain?

we'll see won't we?

He sloped off up the wheelchair ramp instead of the steps. I followed behind him, no kids on the street, still dinner time. The hard modern angles of the Olympic

regeneration and the digital boom gave way to rough
hills and the period buildings of the various museums.
Spotted with paths the mountain appeared around
our feet. Tarmac turned dust. Escalators helped us
ascend level by level as if climbing the folds of the old
man's cloak. We made it to the top, it was a Tuesday,
no fountain below, no music. Relentless beer sellers
roaming between tourists and manhole covers hastily
re-purposed as fridges. Bruto was lucky enough not to
understand, or dog smart enough to deafen himself to
the calls of, "...cerveza, agua, cola, cerveza, beer, beer,
cerveza, agua, cerveza beer." One of the few times I
didn't want to be mute, like I had a choice in the matter.
It was true, the redhead had got me to speak, a little, but
as soon as I stepped out of that apartment, it was gone
again. The moment an individual addressed me, it was
as if the front door closed and I knew without doubt the
keys were inside. There was nothing to be done, I'd had
them, right there in my pocket and yet, click, shit, fuck,
kitchen table, yep. A finger wags across the v of the lips,
the lips stay shut, one points directly at the fold of the
other's mouth, as if willing the individual to see inside
my own, to note the absence of a tongue, of sounds

that can be produced through rattle and hum, shake and vibration. Nada.

We had passed the car park and were heading for the Olympic site. The wide-open marble, concrete and slate, the water, the steps, the columns, placed by the old man on the shoulder. We moved off and over it, upwards towards the graveyards, the urns and boxes in their thousands packed into the cliff. We continued higher into the woods: the castle peering over the brow and hiding just as quickly. Bruto was so resilient: he wasn't quick but he kept shuffling and slaloming upwards. He was on a mission. We stepped off the path, the lights on the road dimming for us, waving us off with a sad orange glow. The forest began to open its eyes to us, the darkness and the trees appearing as one. Bruto made an excellent job of ushering me though. He didn't just amble along at his own height either, plenty of branches he would have cleared and not I, but he was a gent. He stopped and assessed, shuffled to the side.

we'll go through here, its easier.

You're a good dog you know that, a good god damn dog, best I've known.

ah shut up.

I want you to know that though.

but i don't give a shit. i just don't. you're a great guy i like you a whole lot but i don't care what you think of me. i'm a dog i don't think. i do. i need a shit. i go. i want to eat. i eat. i want to get laid. all right I think about that sometimes. but everything else. you're a weight.

Don't say that.

you are. don't be ashamed of it. i like you. i really love you.

He came over and rubbed his muzzle on the inside of my thigh and made a low sigh.

you're the best weight i ever met if that helps.

He sat down and pulled his jowls to pant, but instead dog smiled at me, his eyes blazed in the moonlight, the thinnest of bands catching his cornea, fish gulping for air on a still pond.

I love you too.

i don't care, come on.

We ventured deeper into the forest, I could feel the sea breeze racing at me from the cliffs. The loose rocks offered themselves up at each step now, there was no path, I stumbled plenty, Bruto looked back each time, every bit the mountain goat. I was pleased with the sweater, my footwear had not been so wise, thin house slips folded down into exasperated heels, espadrilles if you will. A heel that had never been erect, refused to hold any purchase on my ankle. I folded it back down and pursued Bruto seemingly with the grip of my toes alone. We came to a cave in the hill. The mouth of which crested the mountain. Bruto walked inside the cave and came back out. He sat at the entrance.

we're good. light a fire.

What would you do without me?

this is about you. without you i wouldn't be here. The way he said it made me blush. I about-faced and hunted for loose bracken. It was plentiful and I made a few trips so we had spares on the side. I had some paper in my pocket, a receipt for shampoo and beer. Nestled in the thinnest twigs, the receipt caught light straight away and took the twigs with them, the sea air waved it on, willed it gently to burn the branches and it was roaring sideways within a minute. Bruto was lying on his front paws looking sadly into the fire. His sadness took on a different form than usual, whatever that might be, between you and me. His sadness looked longingly into the fire as if no matter how many logs I put on it, could never be burned away.

there is something i need to tell you. about yourself. i think you are stuck between the world of the living and the world of the dead. that is the only explanation for our friendship. i've heard tales told of men and hounds, weights and dogs, whatever you want to call it. it's not so common as you think.

Yes.

we can speak to souls you know.

Of course he could. When he said it, I felt I should have been shocked, but here I was being informed of a mystical balance of communication by a Mastiff. It made sense to me that there was more than I could ever understand going on the minds of beasts and men.

I didn't know, but I guess that's cool.

so you must think you are just a soul?

I thought about it deeply, it felt like it could be true, that all the reality was in fact one quick thought, a little scene in an imaginary play. Just an idea on the tip of the writer's pen. A soul floating in the city that resides inside another's mind, an afterthought, just before morning coffee.

No.

that's good that's a very good step. intriguing yes i'll admit.

What does that mean then?

there is only one thing for it. i'll give my soul to you.

The fire roared, I assumed I'd heard him wrong.

Say again.

it's all yours.

What is?

my soul.

He had said it, I didn't want to offend but I had no idea what I would do with a dog's soul. I didn't want it, it sounded dangerous in fact.

Oh you're sweet buddy, but I don't need it. What would I do with two?

He dropped to the floor and wriggled on his back. He didn't laugh but I knew that what was going through his head. Laughing his ass off at the stupid weight.

What's so funny?

He shook himself off, from tail to collar, his ID tags barking together like seals.

that you think you have two.

No, I said I don't need two.

sorry maths was never my strong point.

He pawed at the ground. Two strokes with the claws, I could hear mumbling under his breath.

yeah sorry that's what's funny. you think you have one.

Well of course I do.

He wriggled on his back again.

Stop doing that, be serious.

i'm trying i really am but you know laughter takes the pain away.

He groaned hard and rolled over, the dust and twigs stuck all around his ears and hackles, he smiled at me. He knew that there wasn't much time left. Dust on the hill was a luxury.

Ok come on, you've had your fun with me what are we doing here?

i wasn't joking, i'm really going to give it to you. Frustration overcame me and my insensitivity reared out of the basket.

I already told you I don't know what I would do with it!

Bruto leapt to his feet and placed his paws on either side of my shoulders, he weighted me down and with his snout in my face he growled at me.

    and I told you. you don't have no soul. and you're pretty short on manners too.

He opened his mouth pulled back his jowls and gave me a view of the ivory that could tear my throat out. The liver-spotted roof of his mouth looked like he had wallpapered it with a passing spaniel. I waited with baited breath, the smell of fish hung on his tongue. He burped in my face, nearly dumping a lump of bile on my jersey and dropped to the ground. He was hysterical, he rubbed his back against the rough earth with the clenched teeth of an excellent and enjoyable itch. There are few things on this earth as good as scratching an itch. A great piss after holding out forever. Uncurling your body onto a mattress after a 14-hour flight in economy. Making love. Making love out of nothing but you and another. Forgetting everything and making love. Love and scratching. I could see the redhead in the fire. The mess of her hair laid across the pillow, her face turned away, the blaze of curls watching Bruto squirm in pleasure. I sat down and took my shoes off. I emptied them onto the ground and counted the pebbles that had embedded themselves in the webs of my toes.

Fourteen.

what is?

He was looking at me over his paws, he had been still for
some time it was clear.

Stopped laughing have we?

A brief snort.

some time ago. do you know where your soul
went?

I don't know what you're talking about.

you must have given it away. to someone.

I didn't give anything away.

In the back of my mind I knew I was lying. It seemed
so silly now, with the weight of it all, with him dying in
front of me.

you sure?

Yes. How would I anyway?

what about that girl?

I just met her.

the other one. the one you came here for.

Oh that one.

could you have given it to her?

The feeling in the pit of my stomach grew larger.

why you putting your hand on your belly?

I don't feel so good.

we're getting to the bottom of it. don't stop now. think about that girl, look into my eyes.

I stared at him. I lost myself in his lovely face, he licked his lips absently breaking the space.

yes it's her.

how can you tell?

is it true?

I watched the fire again. I could only see the redhead in the fire. Sleeping in the inferno. I knew that I had given Ana my soul. How I could have done it?

How was it possible?

you loved her. you must have felt that she needed it.

Then what happened to it?

she kept it. you wanted her to.

Vint.

Bruto was sound asleep, bony and unresponsive; the fire gave nothing anymore; I looked into it and thought about lighting it once more. There seemed no point, we had no food and home was only a 30-minute walk. I shook Bruto to wake him, an eye lid moved open.

Come on buddy let's get home.

you have to build the fire again.

No bother, we'll be home in 15 minutes.

i want one last fire. do that for me will you?

I did as I was told, he didn't move a muscle. He looked as if made of stone in the early grey. Once it took light again and started to crackle, he moved inch by inch towards it, the fire creating sounds for his bones waking and moving and living again. He stood to his full four-legged height and shook out his coat. The fire climbed higher for him, I almost believed he fanned it that way.

    i bequeath to you. bequeath, that's right yes?

    Yes I suppose, but wait...

    bequeath to you my only friend … my …

    Not just a weight then?

He stopped, hacked up a big lump of something bloody.
Bruto let the drool hang between him and the ground, he
was tethered.

    … SOUL!

He caught light like he was dowsed in gasoline, the
spittle and the hunk of organ frazzled and curled, charred
on the ground. We said nothing to each other, we did
not move, a buttery thought melted gently in my heart, I
felt it was there, growing, becoming firmer: a cookie in
the hearth, browned, whole. He shrank in front of me;
I felt no sadness that I wasn't able to hug him one last
time. I knew I loved him, I felt inside myself the love
he had for me, I had his soul and yet it was also mine,
unconditional, devoted but ultimately mine. I waited
until the cinders of his remains were unrecognisable. I
waited until late afternoon and I was perished from the
heat. My tongue as dry as sand paper, the temptation to
loll it out the side of my mouth there but the humanistic

inhibitions took over and I resisted the urge to cool myself in that fashion. It made no sense scientifically. I may well feel the soul of the giant mastiff wrapping itself around my heart, but that heart still pumped blood around the vessels and the salt still rose to the surface of the skin to cool my flushes. Hang the tongue out if you want, it might make you feel better, closer to your absent friend but it will make no difference to the temperature inside.

The grey ash rested lightly on itself, it was a dust that defied logic. On a microscopic scale it could hold columns so high and so complex they could be found in Da Vinci's notebooks. With a breeze, the impossible geometry would turn, swirl and ride away to mix with the air. Bruto had now become just such a thing. He had stood there burning, a shell, his form lasted until the breeze of the gods had sucked him off the ridge and inhaled him to their bosom. He was gone, I simply looked like a drunk who had wept too long and wiped too hard at the filth in the pit. The fire blazed in my eyes and all that was left of my great friend was a ring of blackness causing the tramp that hid just below the surface of my leathery face to rise, to wear him like make up, tears of a clown. I had burned my shoes to keep the fire going as long as possible, my shirt also.

Now, I was not looking forward to walking the descent. The stones would be sharp, the twigs sticking into me. The paving, when I had come low enough, would scorch the soles of my feet. Each discomfort would help me not to forget my friend; each sharp pain to sear him into memory. I would never forget him, but I needed to feel him in me longer. The sunburn would flake away like the ash that carried him to the heavens. The blisters would heal. I soon forgot the pain that riddled each step.

The soul began to sing to me in a low gravelly voice. I could hear her voice calling to me, screaming. I could feel her death closely. I had never felt it so close before. She had always felt stolen, she had always felt lost. The Frenchman was not in my mind the way he used to be. He was a bit player. The plot followed a different line. He was not a villain in this new story. He was a passing background *artiste*. The villain was not 'a Frenchman,' the villain had a name, the villain was me. I had let her go. I had invented the Frenchman, ashamed with myself and unable to face my loss. The sun on my back tapped hard to make me turn and face it. I was too cowardly to stare it down and look my name in the face. I had realised whilst looking the other way, that the divination of my soul needed no "Y-shaped" stick to locate it. All souls were one and the same; it was clear to me. I had no idea of the length of this clarity; was it to be afforded me on a temporary basis? It seemed so obvious that I would never be remarkable in any sense. That there would be nothing I would ever do that would make me worthy of a line in a poem. Pointless to give me an epitaph, there was nothing to say. I could not even hear the voices of the hound any more. The snap and bark of a sheepdog playing with his master sounded to me just like any other *weight*. The looks I received from the tourists gazing upon the fountains and the museum looked through me as though I might ask them for money. Nothing but a pair of shorts and door keys separated me from a stray. I was a lucky man.

Vint un.

She waited for me on the cement seats near my front door. She did not look alarmed when she realised it was me. Half of her face expected it, the other half looked on in kindness. She had a folder on her lap, there were clippings escaping the edges. The lettuce too big for her cardboard sandwich.

"What's that?"

I heard my voice crack like an unused oilskin in the window of my throat.

"You speak."

I nodded.

"Long night, I'm tired would you like to come in?"

"Yes I have something to show you."

"I know already."

She stood up and collected her bag over her shoulder.

"I'm not sure you do. I wanted to thank you, for what you did for Barbara."

"Barbara?"

"My dog. You did take my dog to the pound didn't you?"

The redhead.

She tucked her hair behind her ears and smiled.

She looked embarrassed.

"It seems silly to say this, but I know that I need to tell it to you."

"Ok."

"I have been dreaming of you. I have seen you once before and I didn't know it until this morning. It sounds ridiculous, but my dog told me in a dream that you are the man I have been looking for."

She swallowed, shifted her eyes, then narrowed them on me.

"It does a little, yes, but it's no stranger than sharing their souls..."

"You know about that."

"Yes I suppose I do."

We sat back on the bench, in silence for some time.

Finally the redhead looked at me and placed a reassuring hand on mine.

"I'm sorry for your loss."

It came upon me like a burst pipe, welled up in me, I told her everything. The death of Ana, the Frenchman who tried to save her, how I had walked away, how my mind had changed at that moment. Of the years on the wild streets looking for him when he was inside me all along. I held the redhead tight, I whispered how I had let her down. She tried to comfort me by letting me hold her. She told me to let it out. When I had exhausted myself and darkened her shirt with sooty tears, we stood up and made our way to the front door.

"Do you know what is inside here?"

She held the folder.

"It's my story."

"No it's just part of your story. The facts one might say. The facts as the world knows it, it doesn't make them true. We should take this slowly."

I took her at her word, my stewardess for the flight.

"Yes we should."

I reached out my hand.

"Nice to meet you."

"Mi nombre es…"

I leaned in and whispered in her ear. The skin on her cheeks tugged, I could tell that she had smiled. Somewhere above, two souls held each other tight and looked down upon us. I looked up through the buildings as they leaned over us. The windows rolled their eyes upwards in their frames. There was nothing in the sky but colour. I didn't ask for forgiveness, I realised that it too was inside me the whole time. There was a new chapter behind my front door, a page waiting to be turned. Not a full stop, but a new thought, the asterisk on the bottom of the page. An accepted soul, a voice able to be heard.

*